THOUGHTFUL
—PAUSES—

A POLITICAL PHILOSOPHY

D1070338

MICHAEL G. MERHIGE

Fulton Books, Inc.
Meadville, PA

Published by Fulton Books 2017

ISBN 978-1-63338-582-5 (Paperback)
ISBN 978-1-63338-583-2 (Digital)

Printed in the United States of America

To my dear wife and dear family:
You are forever loved and with me.

A political and philosophical writing meant to tweak the reader's interest about the role and function of government, the law and society's place in the higher halls of nationhood that we seek.

FOREWORD

The author realizes that elements of this book will not find favor with even those who might accept much of it. While the aim is to offend no one, it is written with no apology.

TABLE OF CONTENTS

1 SOCIETY AND THE LAW

The ultimate quality and success of a society is not obtained from its institutions, but can only be found in the fabric of its people. It is from their greatness that institutions derive their excellence; and once that fabric is torn, such institutions can only begin to crumble.

Contrary to present practice, society should not be an extension of the law, but the law must be an extension of society. It is society that created the law to act as man's agent; and it is society, through man's evolutionary genius, that created conscience to serve its interest for orderly preservation. It is, therefore, man's conscience, and not the law, that is the true guardian of justice.

The philosophical belief in government of law and not of man is deluding. It is this noble but deluding belief that has brought our legal system to the intellectual dishonesty that ideological justice is more important than truth and justice themselves. Government of law is but government of man, and its quality can only be insured by man's conscience—not his technique.

The moral intuition for justice must not be usurped by some technical rule of law. Adherence to the legal letter will guarantee controlled intellectual dishonesty by those in a position to maneuver the law for their own benefit.

Whenever conscience, that evolutionary invention of society, is replaced by self-serving professional technique, then conscience is diluted by determinations often unrelated to truth and justice. This then cannot be the measure of justice according to the dictates of man's conscience.

Justice can only be determined by man's intuition—that product of society—and not by the courtroom. It is that instinct for justice that must guide man in his quest for truth and equity. Society and its conscience must not allow the technical courtroom to become an actor's stage. Ultimately, man himself, and not his agent the law, is the true guardian of justice. Without his conscience, that instinct for right, we have only a courtroom of fools.

As it was man's instinct for constructive self-preservation that created the law, so must it be his conscience that insures that the law functions as society's servant and not as its master. Society must, therefore, defend its prerogatives to use the law only as its tool to insure justice according to man's instinct for right. Unless he allows moral intuition to prevail, man will only corrupt the institutions that he has established to serve him.

2   CULTURE

That which most significantly defines a country, a nation or any socially organized entity more than anything else is its culture. For it is from the culture that any entity derives its most important ethos—to establish a persona of what is or is not accepted as convention. Culture, this very essence of a nation's being, translates itself into a personality, which dictates how it behaves within itself among its inhabitants and how it acts outwardly towards other countries.

The manner in which we go about our everyday lives comes to us as a byproduct of our culture. Our political, religious, social and economic structures are developed inherently by our culture. So it is then, our culture, which determines the personality of our politics, ways of doing business and social interactions with others. Without a culture, we have nothing to rely on for knowing what our actions should or should not be. Culture, therefore, defines our conscience and lays out what is or is not accepted as convention.

What must follow, therefore, is the realization that the most effective way to change a nation is to change its culture. If one can change that, one has accomplished a feat more permanent than invading a country. One need not risk lives or defeat by making war. Success by force means occupation, which does not alter the culture while the rewards of war have been usually rather short lived.

If culture is the linchpin to any viable society, then a country's strength or weakness can be assessed by finding out what is vulnerable within the specific culture. Once done, a nation is open to a non-violent attack that is decidedly more detrimental long term than an armed invasion. What this so loudly says is, "Change the culture and you change the nation—and possibly forever."

3 DEMOCRACY—THE MOST LOGICAL FORMULA FOR WORLD CONQUEST

Throughout the history of human societies, the basic forms of rule have been laid out, albeit not so well executed, for the civics student for civics student: anarchy—rule by no one; autocracy—rule by one; oligarchy—rule by minority; republic—rule by law; socialism—rule by bureaucracy; democracy—rule by majority.

Many sub-groups exist within these types of rule that run a wide gamut. Notably, all systems are inherently suspect by the people governed—except one. Democracy—that rule by the majority; one man one vote. Abraham Lincoln's "by…for…and of the people" is a system well received for which most choose to embrace without question or hesitation. In pure form, it is a gift for the many to cherish with great numbers of people having much to say about their rule. And so, it is here whereby democracy is allowed to enter to govern without much suspicion and it is here then that democracy poses its greatest danger.

Democracy is the most salable of all governing systems. It, therefore, has an inherent advantage for establishing a foothold within nations when compared to other ruling entities. That government is elected by, and answerable to, the public is a most noble idea. Who would not want democracy—this rule by and for so many? The debate as to whether or not a country is a democracy or a not is but an academic for educational institutions.

Once sold, democracy is wrapped with a warm blanket by the people and embraced as their very own in every way. One does not question democracy's implementation of social, economic, or political systems as one would for other governing models. Society's majority under any other rule can only feel, in degrees, excluded. Under democracy, the citizenry believe themselves to be active players and, to a significant degree, in control—if only psychologically.

What does democracy represent for its people? By definition, it calms the public into a belief that they are part of the process. This, in turn, allows those whose hands steer the helm to have a more controlling, but hidden attitude as to how to implement democracy's rule. Why? Because institutions are perceived to be more sacred and not so corrupted when they are democratic.

With democracy, we understand that the law and press should be accepted as the protectors of democracy and it constituents. Here, then, we have the prime targets for those who would usurp democracy's rule. Once in the hands of exploiters, the law and press can become the anesthetic to deaden the public's senses. Thereafter, it is a matter of time when these self-serving moles begin to hit all virile institutions of power including the military.

This takes us to any country that accepts unquestionably that it has a democracy. Here the door is opened for the oligarchy so unaware to many. If one knows he is ruled by one or a few, then one understands who is in charge and directing. Under a "democratic oligarchy," posing as a democracy, the unsuspecting public contributes to the minority's power. The public, therefore, continues to believe that their representatives are steering the ship.

We have then points to ponder for those who enjoy a democracy and want it to thrive and survive:

- In a democracy, are the laws and the courts products of the majority or of the agents of activists?
- Do the media represent the people or are they instruments of the government of the few?
- Do the elected represent the voters or the lobbyists and their financial contributors?
- Is a Constitution amended by the public or is it is it in the interest of the populous or of the select elite?
- Is government spending and actions openly accountable to the public?
- Has government followed a Constitution in the interest of the majority or the interests a select few?
- Are a nation's institutions influenced or politicized by the majority or the few?
- Is the majority in charge of the country's moral compass or is it in the hands of a few?
- Is the majority or the select elite responsible for the tax structures?

The list is long and need not be detailed here. The conclusion, however, is worth some thought for it sounds the alarm for caution to all democracies. In a democracy, it is not difficult to convey those trappings to allow for it to be insidious and disarming. Add its salability, and democracy becomes an instrument for export and subversion worldwide. It is a most logical form of rule for the oligarch. Dictators are ousted or die, and therefore, lack the perpetual life and consistency of control as the oligarch. No wonder then that democracy is advanced so by government and media today across the globe. We are now in an age of what is called "world economies." Know that there are those who aspire to a "world oligarchy" with democracy being their logical instrument for success. We have already seen the havoc caused by worldwide monetary and financial manipulation. Those that believe that there exists a most satisfactory democracy need to be vigilant. Pure democracy is only an ideal.

4 THE LAW—SOCIETY'S SERVANT OR MASTER

Morality, convention, ethics, and conscience are all the products of society—not the law. It is, therefore, from a contract with civilization that the law gets its beginnings. Remove that social contract from the minds of humanity and the law becomes a weapon principally for abuse and power—not for justice. Allow the law grantors exclusive power to decide right or wrong and you empower the few and remove society's conscience from the equation. The result is a sense of right or wrong, good or bad, according to the deciding legal force. While the court is necessary as a structured guide, it is, in itself, not enough. The court should not be the principle moral instrument. Society's rules of convention are our guiding stars.

There is a case to be made for the comparison of the law being similar, in one aspect, to that of fire. Both have the potential for good but with a danger for harm. As it is with fire, so is it with the law. Both can be used as positive servants or negative masters.

Once a community or nation allows the law to designate itself as society's primary and principle judge of right and wrong, then it is society that is at risk. Whenever the law is accepted as that sole determiner, its abuses become inherent. Thereafter, whatever the powers choose to define is legal and society is left only to accept. We then have legal pretext not for general justice but for selective ones. So where then does convention, that social contract, belong?

Convention or that evolutionary moral compass is an accumulation of centuries of experience by cultures to weather the abuses encountered in humanity's march toward a more civilized day-to-day group existence. What is acceptable and unacceptable behavior has been imbedded through time by trial and error. It is convention that keeps the majority of society's citizenry in proper performance with one another—not the law. The law contrarily allows one to break many those rules society finds unacceptable. For most, the rules of convention or mores of behavior are enough to keep them on the straight and narrow. So it is, therefore, that the law, while it must function for all, is especially necessary for those who have little or no regard for that social contract which the majority hold to and obey.

When a community agrees to entrust its definitions and rules of right and wrong almost exclusively to select professionals, then society delivers its prerogatives freely into the hands of the self-anointed. It behooves the governed to understand that legal is not always right nor right always legal. The law must have its place and be followed but society should impose the guidelines—not the reverse. This balance cannot be maintained if the adage "government of law and not of men" is accepted blindly without question. To quote from this author's Society and the Law, "Government of law is nothing but government of men." Otherwise, by whom or what is the law—if not by men?

One might view what has become the "social contract" for behavior to that of repositioning a huge vessel. It requires much time and great effort to effect any noticeable change. The law, on the other hand, requires little to be redirected or remolded. A mere revision in the make-up of the court will create 180 degrees of change in a social structure. Major legal decisions are subject to change merely by a one vote difference. Consensus, therefore, is anything but guaranteed when the law is at work. In righteous or just hands, it is a most cherished instrument—but only an instrument. In the hands of the mal-intentioned, it is a weapon to be challenged at best and feared at worst.

Is it the law or ethics that keeps one from entering church in a bikini or openly visiting a neighbor's home for a tryst? What would we be without this time-honored ethos? We would be a lesser culture, not because of the law, but for the absence of established convention. It is convention that keeps the majority legitimate rather than legal and it is convention that allows us to go about our everyday business without trying to infringe on another's peaceful existence.

The law, no doubt, has its necessary place, but all the laws and policing in the world would not control a full time felonious populace void of any inbred ethic or conscience. So it is humanity's ethic that allows us not to trample on each other in our daily routines. When we fail to come to another's aid—be it a young woman in distress or an elderly one who has fallen—what stops us more than not is the fear that the law can punish for giving aid. We dare to assist because of conscience and dare not because of legal concerns.

The law, therefore, must be a reflection of society and not the driving force. If not, whatever the court decides must be accepted not as only legal but as correct and just. The assumption here is that conscience, that right or wrong, is exclusively the prerogative of a select "legal" entity. Ethics then takes a back seat and the court's findings are tantamount to true justice.

It is in the nature of things that to institutionalize is to politicize. So it is with the law. This, in time, will only create an inherent weakness in the legal system. When politics is introduced, the guarantees for justice diminish. Institutions tend to make themselves inviolate or, at best, become self-protective and politically selective. Too much law will surely lead to too much abuse.

The definitive philosophy on what the law should be is a masterful writing by Frederic Bastiat and titled, not surprisingly, "The Law." This classic for legal justice was written in the mid-nineteenth century just prior to Bastiat's death in 1850—the year it was published. Of all his endeavors, none defines Bastiat more than this work. To understand Bastiat, here is to discern the just and true role of law within society and not of society within the law. His premise is that legal justice can only be insured with a minimal amount of judicial activism. This is crucial since Bastiat's law is more beneficial when employed as a last resort than as a panacea for societal control. Sadly, this writing is not commonly presented for study in our halls of learning. Given the supplanting of convention by the law in society, this paucity of distribution and the teachings of Bastiat's work are neither surprising nor unexpected. The result is the loss of meaning and importance for modern civilization's social contract.

5 WHAT DEMOCRACY OR DEMOCRATIC FREEDOM IS NOT

This section is not intended to demean democracy's freedoms, but to point out where a few of its weaknesses may lie at the moment.

While democratic free forms of government are many things, they are not:

Where censorship is called political correctness

Where merit takes a back seat to social and economic engineering

Where equality is an agenda and substituted for equity

Where the public is finessed to vilify select religious groups but not others

Where censorship is selectively imposed by the ruling class

Where the government and media perpetually preach of impending threats only to send its youth to war, but careful to avoid military conscription

Where its leaders are elected and influenced by money and media while the public is led to believe its vote counts and democracy exists

Where government officials are not held accountable

Where the financial institutions create periodic financial havoc but are inviolate of punishment

Where media, government, and major corporations are aligned but at the public's expense

Where qualified students are refused admission to universities so that less qualified ones can receive preference

Where quotas are instituted not for equity but for agenda

Where illegal immigrants are not only allowed to come, but encouraged and assisted to remain

Where nations do not hesitate to invade defenseless countries but avoid war with others with greater threats capable to retaliate

Where the military elite are promised high paying jobs with government, media and large corporations to peddle influence and justify the making of war

Where residents are judged as threats not for their background or actions but for their ethnicity

Where the media propagandizes and imposes its view rather than reports

Where invading countries and overthrowing their leaders is invariably done in the name of instilling democracy and freeing the populous

Where financial bailouts in the millions are for corrupt, abusive banks

Where a nation's Constitution is selectively ignored

Where oligarchs and lobbyists are the main influence in government

Where politicians answer to influence peddlers, not the people

Where much of the populous continue to believe that they have a democracy

Where the criminal elite easily find refuge

Where congressional and other hearings are performed in secret not for national security but to hide wrong doings from the public

Where the public elect the candidates, but it is the lobbyists that the elected represent

Where the media dictate who our allies and enemies are and are not

6 THOUGHTFUL PAUSES

The facts of history are with us but for a fleeting instant. Whatever of them that are not captured at the moment becomes only eternal folklore.

No law, no matter how equitably written, will secure justice when implemented by dishonest men. No law, no matter how poorly written, will deter justice when guarded by men of good will.

The history of governments is a history of arrogance, excesses, deceit, and dishonesty. It matters not what form as all governments possess these vices.

Truth—it has a deep underlying virtue. It protects the unaware, the innocent, and the unsuspecting. It defines the lowest depth of a matter, thus making ascent possible. Truth promotes healing, understanding, and trust. It removes doubt, suspicion, and speculation—all factors that hinder stability and progress.

Intellectual or philosophical dishonesty can be more costly than material dishonesty. Religion's effects on humanity are more cultural and political than religious. That which is physical is more with reality than that which is mental.

Beware the cult-like group for when it turns it does so in masse like a frenzied school of fish.

Those who aggrandize war are too often bullies or cowards.

Government is political and all that it touches becomes to one degree or another affected politically.

Media's most effective power is mostly derived from the people unable to think for themselves.

Democracy can only function if its people function.

One person can be many people.

War is the ultimate lie to cover all lies.

Elite media's principal endeavor is to sell their manipulative agenda.

Mainstream media and religion have much in common. They both too often preach myth.

A sleeping populace is satisfied with its government. The ones awake are never at ease.

Governments should be run by passing rather than by career politicians.

No weapons are as destructive as a monopolistic and manipulative media.

Modern media's penetration into our homes and minds is without parallel.

Beware the media, which take it upon themselves to be the courtroom for judicial process.

Beware the destructiveness of a mainstream media that answers to and are elected by no one.

The oldest and most lucrative endeavors for making money are nestled within the practices for banking and religion.

Almost never accept a government's numbers as correct.

The people's responsibility in a democracy is to continually hold the government's feet to the fire.

It is wrong to spy against ones government but not wrong to monitor it ever so closely.

To be politically correct is to be censored.

When getting at the truth one should know the source's bona fides.

The more there is of government the less there is of freedom.

Politics is a disgusting profession when invariably controlled by politicians and not by statesmen.

Politicians are the counterparts of prostitutes. Politicians sell themselves, however, on a grander scale while there is a limit to how much prostitutes cost.

To entrust government to monitor itself is to entrust a thief to leave an unprotected wallet untouched.

It is not a democracy when the same group too often monopolizes the players and the conversation.

More important to the success or failure of a political system are the leaders who control it rather than the system itself.

There are two ways to steal—legally and illegally. Legally, it is safer and much more lucrative.

Politics should be a calling not a racket.

The media should report, not preach, cover-up or invent.

War planners, elite, and their offspring should be the ones to lead on site the battlefield charge.

Those who cannot read between the lines should choose carefully what they peruse.

There appears to be little difference, if any, between how believers and non-believers accept knowing their end is near.

Institutions should be erected to serve mankind - not for mankind to serve its institutions.

"Lobbyism" is as detrimental to the public interest as "Satanism."

I see no correlation between man's scientific knowledge of the universe and mankind's certainty about his religion.

Media dictatorship is every bit a dictatorship.

Public discussion is used too often to cover up private practices and has become a way of life with our politicians.

Drunken sailors do not hold a candle to governments in the spending column.

The general populace is much better cared for when its leadership is well-meaning and of good will.

If anyone has forfeited the right to claim itself protectorate of press freedom it is big media.

When money and media are paramount for being elected then a pseudo-democracy is what the people will get.

Beware those who parade themselves the eternal victim.

The best place for the undeserving to get what they want is by getting a lawyer and going to court.

There exists no democracy when the elected must repeatedly answer to the same group of elites.

Beware the patriot who enlists others to fight his battles.

Patriotism is not about how much noise one can make.

One should know the difference between a patriot and a warmonger.

Discerning patriotic groups and their leaders from pseudo-ones is vital for a nation's welfare.

Advertising's success demonstrates our preference for good news rather than the truth.

The biggest crooks are bankers. Present times have shown us that a barter system would better serve many of us than one of banking.

Government understands it need not illegally confiscate property. It has only to tax it.

When media and government have the same agenda then look elsewhere for the truth.

A misinformed/uninformed populous will neither deserve nor keep its democracy.

Celebrations should be for positive events—not for deriving joy from others' misfortunes.

Politicians running for office will promise the world to get there and once in office will do anything to stay.

Politicians and bankers have the common goal to put their hands in your pockets.

A most effective way to distort history for the masses is by making movies.

Ultimately, money is what rules.

A "mediagarchy" can be every bit a ruling power as any other dictatorship with damage more potent as their "tenure in office" is limitless.

With its unbridled imagination, the media have little need of worthy news to report.

War medals are the cheapest form of payment to the battlefield fighter. Only a select few combat medals have value while the rest are there for meaningless parade.

When watching "accurate" media interviews, know that the interviewed are averse to bare their true thoughts with microphones and cameras hovering in their faces.

When the whistleblowers are the ones punished, then you know your country is in trouble. A country that feeds on others will ultimately feed on itself.

Balance of power is the securest instrument for avoiding war.

It matters not the system of government as corrupt politicians practice corrupt politics that create and perpetuate dishonest government.

Cowards, dreamers, the ignorant, and politicians aggrandize war.

Beware the banker.

Whoever said, "Exaggeration is a form of lying" must have had politicians in mind.

Advertising is brainwashing.

Democracy's children must grow up quickly to protect themselves from their guardian politicians.

To believe a politician most often is naïve, but to do so during election time is insane.

When money and media are what win elections and lobbyists flourish then democracy exists only in the minds of wishful thinkers.

The expression "Do as I say, not as I do" was written with politicians in mind.

The media will critique everyone but themselves.

When a government enforces its laws for the people but not for itself then it's time for its replacement.

Democracy presupposes a responsible and discerning populous to succeed.

A people that will give the media a free pass will in time forfeit their freedom.

Beware the political media.

When the public can discern what the press reports from what it ignores then it can better judge media's veracity.

A public that will swallow whatever it is fed by the media will inevitably suffer information poisoning.

An over taxed and over regulated citizenry have no democracy.

There are no weapons as explosive to their targets as information planted within the minds of men.

When the guarding of democracy is left to anyone but the people, then democracy will be no longer.

Beware a society rife with organizations for they too often exist at the expense of the general public.

The voter who believes his job is done when casting his ballot is like the mother who believes her work is over after giving birth.

Big media insure big manipulation of information.

When mainstream media are a monopoly then freedom of the press becomes a self-protection mechanism for its elite.

Left unchecked, a country's rotten leadership will produce the proverbial apple barrel.

Ubiquitous congressional hearings are almost exclusively for public consumption. They are meant to engage the populous but designed generally to lead nowhere.

An electronic age that so greatly facilitates speed and efficiency so too allows for corruption to increase and flourish exponentially.

There exists no true freedom without freedom of speech for all.

Freedom of speech is for everyone—not just for the press, the government, and the politically correct.

Politically correct promoting media are as dangerous an obstacle to freedom as a monopolistic government.

Monopolistic media guarantee the public one way information. Debate and outside perspectives are mostly non-existent and the only interests served are for those who pump out their one-way bias.

Liability suits are to the uninsured what alligators are to ducks.

A politically correct driven society is insidiously devoid of freedom.

Those who apologize for statements deemed politically incorrect are intimidated souls to be pitied.

Freedom of the press too often results in denial of freedom to anyone who might be big media's target.

There exists no weapon more potent than big media's monopoly for controlling the minds and freedoms of the masses. They intrude, embellish, exaggerate, bully, prevaricate, invent, ignore, target, intimidate, politicize, and propagandize to foment their elite agendas. A population can recognize the power of physical weapons but cannot discern big media's destructiveness. All sectors of society are in fear of their attack and yet are impotent to respond in kind. Today, absolute freedom of speech is their domain and theirs alone.

Politics is the highest form of deceptive salesmanship.

Whoever controls the message to the public controls the minds of the masses.

Democratic political dynasties are more a product of the media than anything else.

Agenda driven media are freedom's most dangerous enemy.

The more the law dictates the less society functions.

Let the war-makers taste a bit of another's gunpowder.

Scapegoating belongs to the exploiters.

Those who present themselves as all things to all men are mostly unto their own self-interests.

Too often, there appears to be little room at the top for people of conscience.

Democracy lies only in the minds of the naive when money and media are the principal ingredients for electing and lobbying politicians.

A media operating void of boundaries is undeserving of untethered freedom.

Where humanity has evolved the least is in its care and understanding of the mentally ill.

Too often, suicide is the result of our primitive treatment of the mentally ill.

Psychiatry's contribution to modern day mental health issues is as useful as snake oil and witchcraft.

All religions come with their own bias.

The parallel to the expression "my dad can whip your dad" is "my religion is better than your religion."

Those who promote political correctness are the enemies of freedom of speech and thought. They hide behind a facade of correctness to stifle debate and control their own agendas.

Too often, freedom of speech is guaranteed solely when one is politically correct.

Social censorship infringes on freedom not nearly as much as having to be politically correct.

New releases by big media of prior unreported past events and deeds by personalities invariably carry with them media's untimely and purposely-skewed agendas.

And who is there to report on and expose the media?

In a democracy, the people must be the caretakers of good government and should allow neither to be unaccountable.

Any political system is capable of good government and bad government.

Departments of Defense for aggressive nations should be known as War Departments.

If a corrupt leader is difficult to remove, a corrupt system is even more so.

One's success should not be overly enjoyed nor for too long. The top of the heap is the most enticing target.

Bankers provide their services mainly to hold and use your money.

Investment bankers are the sharks that swim in the seas of money.

The nationalistic self-described exceptional is the product of a culture strutting in arrogance and deluded by ignorance.

Too often, too many are more captivated by the noise than the substance.

When freedom to question or criticize is in any way abridged, then freedom already is lost.

Big media are at best just another man's opinion; and at worst, just another man's agenda.

I know of nothing so insidiously dangerous and threatening to freedom as unbridled big media's ability to consistently seek and receive the people's unquestioning trust.

The balance of power most crucial to a nation's freedom is the people and their vigilance against all combined governmental and institutional enterprises.

Just as not all dictatorships are despotic so it is that neither are all democracies benevolent.

Advertising is an efficient way to create an inflated or false value.

Beware the clicks of perennial advisors, experts and councilors who hang around those career politicians found at every level. They serve only themselves and not the people.

Be hesitant to accept heroes and saviors at face value.

Freedom of speech and movement are essential to the common good.

Too often, one can count on the media to report only its side of the story.

Too often, too many rely on and accept what their government and big media feed them.

Monopolizing the people's attention and controlling their focus is a compelling weapon of big media.

Politically engaged media appearing neutral are not worthy of trust.

Control the media, the message, the mind, the people, and the system.

In a democracy, when the controlling majority of people realize their power is diminished only when their pockets or bellies become empty, then it is not this form of government that they deserve.

The key to understanding agenda media's deceit is to discern the where and why of their focus.

Heroes and cowards are not absolute, but often depend on circumstances and a mind-set at the time.

Today's hero can be tomorrow's coward and vice-versa.

Whoever coined "exaggeration is a form of lying" surely had advertisers in mind.

The financier even controls the industrialist.

Beware the global centrists as they seek world domination of all people.

Know the difference between sincere calls for patriotism and the self-agenda flag wavers.

Know the difference between movies that entertain and those that propagandize social and political agendas.

Society must allow no room for exceptions in securing due process of law for every person.

Politicians who sell their souls for money and power should not be left alone as too many will sell their country in the process.

The most dangerous monopoly is the one that controls mass communication fed to the public.

A working democracy presupposes a great deal of self-discipline and awareness on the part of the governed.

The old adages are time and experience tested.

The citizenry would do well to know that dictator governments come in all sizes, shapes, and numbers.

Truth is the byproduct of conscience and lack of conscience causes truth to suffer.

A news media that habitually omits both sides of the story should not be trusted for its reporting practices.

Warriors who are good statesmen and statesmen who are good warriors seldom come along.

A most convenient activity for many believers is the foisting of their religion on others while having no intention of practicing it themselves.

The idea of a centralized global government should never be allowed to happen until all governments and its people can respect all human life as dearly as their own.

Centralized governments and organizations produce centralized controls that are inherently dangerous to individual freedom.

There are no wars that produce lasting peace.

The value of "word of mouth" depends on who is doing the talking.

The nation's "sheep" are ever so ready to march in step to the politically correct suggestions of government and media, if for no other reasons than to look good and feel good.

Take care not to be a party to injustice. On the contrary, be the enemy of it.

Beware the instigators who commit a purposeful vile act so that the public response will be to give them what they would not have been afforded otherwise.

Any elected, self-titled "democratic" government without transparency is anything but democratic.

It is best not to judge one's government position as being all bad and another's as being all good until the tables can be reversed.

Too often the press has a way of reporting its stories not for wanting to deliver the truth, but for the purpose of swaying public opinion its way.

Centralization of the whole is invariably at the expense of the parts.

Individual freedom will suffer whenever governments centralize for control rather than for efficiency as they would have their subjects believe.

Government and media should find it difficult to coexist comfortably if individual freedom is to flourish.

The control of a society's targeted public and private leadership is to control its citizens. Another is the political and social control through the media.

Too many would rather focus their attention upon comfortable untruths rather than on hard realities.

Too many would rather believe a high-powered snake oil salesman than listen to veritable speakers.

Military parades are there for a purpose of mostly enhancing the young wanting to fight and die.

Let the soldier decide to make war and let the politician go to fight it.

Parades and medals are society's rewards to the maimed, the fallen and their dear ones.

It does not always follow that people who accomplish great things necessarily lead great lives.

The greater the population there is, the richer the elite.

There is no market for the meek and helpless.

Know with whom you should shake hands and with your other hand over your wallet.

Marketing and advertising go hand in hand to reach into your pocket.

A democracy that fails to function as such sooner or later leads to anything but.

Words of wisdom too often are only captured by the ears of a few.

One of the lowest forms of wolf pack actions is becoming whatever it takes to fill an agenda.

A democratic society with government and mass media having a common philosophy is anything but a democracy.

A most taxing element to a democratic system is the oligarchs. Their reign is too often recurrent while politician and bureaucrats can come and go.

A nation's most valuable resource is its people.

The quote "government of law and not of men…" is nothing more than government of men.

Conscience is humanity's inherent mandate for good. Without conscience, the law will no doubt be used as an instrument for manipulation.

The expression "talk is cheap" is anything but when employed by politicians.

Ones perspective of war is colored by ones being at a desk or in the trenches and whether one is on the giving or receiving end.

A wounded soldier can speak more about the effects of war than all the politicians, moviemakers, and historians.

Statesmen speak for the ages while politicians chatter for the moment.

Let the politician fight the war and let the soldier do the speaking at the gravesite of the fallen.

There is no warm home coming for the dead soldier, nor is there any parade for his loved ones.

It is not a heroic war when it is a "turkey shoot." In such cases, let us not celebrate the victory or the victor.

Celebrations are not long lasting after the battles and wars have ended.

Too often, the religious certainty of zealots fix their beliefs unrelated to and beyond matters pertaining to their religion.

What big media wants you to know is that they dig at endlessly. What big media does not want you to know is that they ignore or manipulate. Sadly, reality for too many becomes what they are fed daily by the media.

In a democracy, when freedom is lost, the people should look to themselves first when attaching accountability.

Politicians support and promote many "beneficial causes" with the primary intention being to benefit themselves.

Freedom of the press is not and should not be considered above freedom of the people.

And who is there to investigate and report on the press?

It is as important, if not more so, to be as skeptical of media reporting as it is to question statements of politicians.

A monopolistic and agenda driven free press is anything but a protector of the truth for the benefit of a democratic society.

When the people believe without question in their mainstream media they subject those who would challenge the press to threats of social and even legal blackmail.

Freedom does not usually dissipate all at once nor by itself, especially in a democracy.

Big monopolistic media is no better than a dictator government. Both are of one voice for the purpose of insuring their agendas and power.

In anything political, too often, there are hidden agendas behind the rationales offered to the public.

A democracy cannot survive rampant infections of hypocrisy and lies.

The finest legal systems still respond best to money and influence.

If war is, at times, a short-term solution, it is never so for long.

Life is a journey appearing long and winding that at destination's end seemed ever so short.

The advertiser and the politician have much in common. They both speak to their markets in their language of unbridled hyperbole.

Politicians and hypocrisy are never more in tune than when the cameras are rolling and the microphones are on.

Children's circuses and adults' congressional hearings are difficult to distinguish one from the other.

Monopolistic media control is more insidious and lasting than that of government or any other institution.

The purest state of equality is when a successful rich man and an unsuccessful poor man lay side by side on their death beds.

Centralizing the world community is the ultimate recipe for a cuisine of conquest and control.

When given the choice between having enemies or masters, choose enemies.

Politicians excel in offering empty promises to the public while delivering results to special interests.

The public's needs are rarely on the same page with the politicians' agendas.

A one world government will make it simpler for one world slavery.

Allow the door to open for the honest, but take care to keep it shut for the dishonest.

Beware of those who like to feed their prepared dishes to others, but almost never partake of their own cooking.

There is no correlation between an existence of God and man's invention of religion.

A gullible public is the ripe fruit for picking by government and media.

Too many notables cast by history for their admirable qualities, in truth, resemble little or none of them.

Control the money, control the media, and thus, control the institutions that control the population.

Too often, attention that is mal-focused produces unjust results that entrap the innocent and allow the guilty to run free. Scapegoating especially comes to mind.

A one sided agenda-driven media not only demeans and diminishes "freedom of the press," but consequently places freedom itself in jeopardy.

There will always be young uninitiated followers to fight the wars of older scheming power brokers whose aims have nothing to do with defending country or the innocent.

It is not important to be of the left or the right, but only to be truthful and just.

Government is the people's business in a democracy or it will not remain as such.

Government belongs to the people en masse. It belongs not to groups, organizations, or those who are elected. A people who fail to grasp this fundamental concept will be ruled by elements not of the people's interests.

When government and media are driven by the same forces, then freedom is but a distant ideal.

When a people accept to be politically correct, they forfeit their freedom to speak and act.

Too much law means too little freedom.

Beware when the law protects or is applied only to some.

When a people lose the ability to rule for themselves, they guarantee their rule by others who do so not in the people's interests.

A government that will over regulate will present an expensive tab for an inferior meal.

Governments cannot and should not impose equality for its citizenry. What they should strive for is equity.

The citizenry should take care to be forever aware of the government's tendency to rule its people and not to serve them.

A wise and benevolent dictator brings the most efficient and equitable system of government to its people.

A working democracy without direct majority participation by an educated and reasonable populous is an ideal more than a reality.

Those elected by the people are put there to represent all and not to curry favor to select groups.

Beware of organizations. Too many are there as wolf packs to impose their will and take power for a myriad of selfish reasons.

International bankers have always been power broking rascals. The last thing on their minds is to hold your money for safe keeping.

Democracy is not for the naïve, disinterested, gullible, or lazy.

Lawmakers should be adjudicated by the same legislation that they write for the public.

Most crucial to government regulation is the one which demands and insures that the regulators are held accountable.

When democracy's people are dissatisfied with their government, but not sure of whom to blame, they should vote out the leadership.

War is a beast that comes in many sizes, shapes, and patterns. All come with a cruel destructiveness.

Most revolting about wars are the architects who invariably are never the victims of their actions.

Never take seriously the movie makers and advertisers. They deal in anything but reality and, too often, have in mind only to influence.

If the same people are always writing the history books, then what we have is agenda folklore.

The super patriot is often merely an over-zealous bully looking for a lame excuse to inflict harm upon someone else.

When the law becomes a political instrument, then it no longer protects its people.

A population that is only attentive to the news of big media will not be able to discern its agenda reporting and will, too often, be misinformed or uninformed.

A true patriot looks to defend his country from harm and searches not for excuses to attack targets for hidden agendas.

The history of humanity is a history of unbridled gullibility by the many that are ruled by lies and deceit from those in power. Nothing has changed and it matters not the political system.

People tend to accept whatever big media offers.

We know what wars the elite media prefer and which ones they don't by the way they report them.

When we support a senseless war to send our sons and daughters with no conscription or imminent national danger, then we have little reason to mourn when they do not return alive or whole.

The general public would rather be entertained by production news from major media networks, which too often produce propaganda rather than reporting relevant news from balanced sources.

The people should understand that national security is a two-edged sword to be used for the public good. It is not to be used to allow government and the elite to limit freedom, impose undue restrictions, and withhold information.

A government that keeps too many secrets from its citizens is a government that should not be trusted.

The prerogatives of the elite and the public's general welfare will invariably be at odds.

When freedom of speech is not afforded to each individual, then the people should never allow any group or organization to self-impose this freedom upon itself with media being no exception.

We should know the faults of our nation in order to better understand how the world views us and how we view ourselves.

Beware those who want to promote their agendas by celebrating events—even adverse ones.

Hypocrisy is countenanced in matters of diplomacy among nations. It should not be acceptable between governments and its people.

The super patriot, as a self-appointed guardian of his country, is a threat to the nation's citizenry who question government policy.

Pity the people who are represented by politicians who righteously and publically denounce to reporters crimes against the innocent, but who do nothing else to protect them.

Advertising is to exaggeration what bread is to butter.

The politician starts the war, the soldier fights it, and the populous morns it.

War is that sad truthful consequence that is borne out of the hypocrisy of politicians.

Arm the politicians and let them kill and maim each other so that the people will go before the cameras and make glorious speeches.

The victor and the vanquished will eventually switch positions and the consequence is invariably more of the same.

The politician will cover his weaknesses by conjuring up reasons for war while the statesman will do whatever he can to avoid it.

Be sensitive not to incorporate as a nation those habits for which you despise of other nations.

When critiquing the enemy's war tactics, take care not to overlook in your nation the same ones for which you fault the adversary.

Be ready to defend that which is just even when unpopular and challenge injustice no matter how well accepted.

It should come as no surprise that people ponder ever so seriously the meaning of life as it strikes them most significantly—when they know death is imminent.

Holidays are now more an excuse to vacation and shop rather than a way to celebrate ones religion or remember those who have served or passed.

Beware the self-appointed who profess to make better a person or nation's situation when their true objective too often is to promote self-interest.

Freedom of the press is no more an absolute freedom than freedom for the individual. To assume otherwise is to accept media's self-appointed dictates to operate at will and create a double standard for them alone.

Special interest groups are as much a danger to a democracy as any looming adversary.

The will of the people in a democracy is not enough to insure a fair and just rule. Access to and control of the government must be universal for its citizens, or government will belong to the very few and democracy will be in name only.

The general public will most often come around to accept whatever social and political agendas big media pushes as their priority.

Wherever political correctness is allowed to thrive, free speech and democracy will then struggle to breathe.

The people's freedom is not selective. It cannot be just for some and not for others. To think otherwise is to dupe oneself about celebrating democracy.

Simplistic thinkers are the fertilizer for those who are intent upon manipulating the thoughts and actions of a nation.

When the people become dissatisfied with their presumed democratic government and continue to elect the same persons to represent them, then it is the people themselves who are mostly at fault for their dissatisfaction.

Lobbyists and organized election money contributors stand in the way of democratic government. To allow for their participation is to make a mockery of the political selection process and the right to vote.

Democracy defines the elected as being those chosen to represent and carry out the people's wishes. When they do otherwise, the people should look to themselves to correct this malfeasance or realize they have chosen to walk away from this precious freedom.

News agencies restrict the news in totalitarian countries while news agencies fabricate their information in countries with "open societies." In both cases, the people are too often uninformed and misinformed.

In a democracy, the governed should take care to do some of the governing and those who are governing should be the governed whenever necessary.

There may be no greater farce within a democracy than when its people have no awareness of their government's doings and yet continue to believe the information they are fed.

The people should hold their governments accountable for their actions just as responsible parents require good behavior from their children.

When questioning why entertainers and athletes are mainly society's heroes, simply look to the media who promote them at the expense of the scientists, care givers, educators, and so many other contributors to our well-being.

A system which relies mostly on lobbyists, money, and media for electing its political leaders cannot be expected nor trusted to represent and act judiciously for the people. To believe otherwise is naïve and self-deluding.

Freedom of the press cannot be accepted as an absolute. To invest it with absolute powers threatens the freedom of us all outside its circle.

Too often, big media have the habit of reporting that a tree fell in the forest when it didn't and ignore a tree falling when it did.

If we are now seeing that the universe is unstable, why would we believe that humans or anything else belonging to it would be the exception?

Big media's overwhelming access into our minds makes them the most powerful and influential of entities in our lives.

No matter how bright or dim, common or uncommon, famous or unnoted, we all end our journey in the same place and fashion.

The first amendment pertains to a "reporting" press not an "agenda" media. Nor should the press be the one to define itself.

Big government and individual freedom are like roommates forced to live together but who will never get along.

Big government, big media, and big business in no way can be for the common interest of the people.

The ubiquitous debating between liberals and conservatives about matters of justice should be focused on having those in authority getting it right.

If freedom is not an absolute for organized society, then this less than absolute condition should also pertain to the press, which would have us to believe otherwise.

If war is invariably a solution for peace, are we to assume that peace is almost always the justification for war?

When the controlling media come continually with one-sided opinions, then they are not a free press but merely political influence peddlers.

And who is there to judge the elite media who are more to judging rather than reporting?

It would seem that the actions of a government toward its people are what count and not the titles nor the descriptions of the governmental systems.

When a country's government chooses to send its sons and daughters to be maimed or die for unjust and unnecessary wars then the people must question where the real enemies reside.

Humanity's propensity to forget is no more evident than when seeing humanity's willingness to ignore the consequences of past wars while entering into the next.

Conscience, that built-in breaking system, acts to restrict the actions of those influenced by it while providing others not so influenced with predatory advantages. Thus, folklore aside, the good do not always prevail over the bad.

Judge those by their actions and not by their titles nor by their speeches.

Too many notables in the news are not what they seem. Take care not to accept what a favorable press has done for a never ending array of so many celebrated undeserving.

Freedom of the press when written in the Constitution was freedom to print—not to intrude on others rights, fabricate, cover-up, intimidate, or influence legal proceedings.

What we, as a nation, teach to our children at home and students in schools defines us.

Our air waves should be filled with notables as fine examples of good character and model living.

We should choose our own heroes and not those so often promoted by politicians and the media.

If "power corrupts and absolute power corrupts absolutely" then know that money corrupts even more so and its power is longer lasting.

In the interest of good health we should learn to know when we are being treated by someone from the medical profession and when our treatment is by someone from the medical industry.

All governments, friendly, unfriendly or otherwise, suffer some of the same vices. None should be revered unconditionally nor be accepted for having carte blanche over the will of the people.

The elite have wealth, power, influence, and more unrestricted freedom than those outside their clique. They invariably take much more from society than they give notwithstanding the continuous and often undeserving positive press coverage they receive for their "charity."

When the general population begins to second guess or pre-analyze what they want to say publically, then they no longer enjoy the pleasures of a free society.

Big media too often are tailored to keeping the masses misinformed and uninformed. And what could be a better way to keep them so?

A society is only free when the people take care to insist upon it being so.

Turning one's head or closing one's mouth when confronted with injustice is safe, but cowardly and rips at the heart of individual freedom.

With a dictatorship, the captain is at the helm. In a democracy, take care, the lobbyists and advisors are not the ones steering the vessel.

Patriotism is an action to be taken with pride and loyalty. It is not to be used as a verbal exercise so to look good or feel self-impressed.

When media and politicians are more vocally patriotic than the soldier's actions, then it is time to call back the troops from their questionable engagements and replace them with the former.

For the ones unschooled in fiscal matters, those bankers and other financial advisors are to be trusted only with their own monies.

Even free societies will not endure when money and media are controlled by a select few.

For the ones at home, war is not such a bitter pill to swallow when the battle is always on the enemy's own turf.

A press that wishes to manipulate the court room has no interest in the workings of justice.

It is simpler for the people to know the obvious despotic leader, but more difficult for them to see the hidden oligarchs who lurk in the wings of government and who are as much controlling and exploitive as any dictator.

The dictator's grasp over those he rules is easy to see. The oligarch's control is not so obvious and more insidious.

When the influential are wanting for that which is not only undeserved, but also unobtainable then their next move is to hire a lobbyist.

Whoever said that "there is no free lunch" forgot to include all other meals.

Modern media are so encompassing that the receiver had better know about who is doing the reporting in order to see when the journalistic agendas are running rampant.

Media pressure has no peer.

There exists a vast difference between press freedom and press abuse and it behooves the public to know the difference.

The practice of awarding honors to those undeserving of their recognition comes at the expense of those who have earned it and is a fraud of the worst kind.

War does not necessarily make the man, but man is certainly what makes the war.

Neither the hero nor the coward act at all times in their life consistently or in accordance with their reputation.

Everyone's definition of religion is unique and unto each individual's belief—no matter the house of worship to which they belong.

Any similarity between the press as it should exist and as it operates is a figment of one's own imagination.

A manipulative public media that will influence rather than report is a poison that infects the minds of well too many people.

It is important to understand the necessity to identify correctly a premise. For it is from a premise that all other conclusions are arrived at and built upon for any given subject.

Beware of those who specialize in the tactic of falsifying the premise of any information or event in order to promote their agenda. Once done, their intention to deceive is easily foisted upon a naïve and undiscerning public.

Elite media's principal endeavor is to brainwash. Anyone taken in by them can only see the world through distorted lenses.

Freedom of the press is but a wisp of smoke when controlled by elite oligarchs in league with all facets of business and government.

Politicians who reputedly wrap themselves within the flag are anything but statesmen.

Many interpretations of democracy come encapsulated with deceit.

The elite media take care and pride in promoting to the public phony entertainers, politicians and wealthy politicos. Sadly, the public, in turn, willingly accept this iconic fraud perpetrated against them for money and to promote political and social agendas.

The promotion of entertainers has less to do with talent and more to do with riches for the business entities surrounding them.

The promotion and vending of art has become a facile means for legal theft.

Too often, the elite media present their reporting as being in the interest of the political, social, and economic disenfranchised when, in fact, they are only in pursuit of their own agendas.

The press has become too often a propaganda machine for its own agenda.

Common popular history is an agenda driven history manipulated by elite political interests.

Democracies are not for the lazy, disinterested, or faint of heart.

Whenever past notables are resurrected in the media, it is invariably for money and the person of interest is merely the vehicle.

With a democracy, if the people do not understand that they are in charge to control the government, then their democracy is one they will not keep.

The farther one is from shore the more difficult the endeavor to swim back. So it is also with runaway government spending.

With governments, bad habits have a manner of becoming a way of life.

Those who are in the business of controlling governments will invariably opt for centralized government.

A politician's promise should carry the same value as a gigolo's request for one's hand in marriage on a romantic evening.

Wars are decidedly matters of perspective. They matter greatly when people are on the receiving end and matter less when they are not.

There exists nothing as perpetually divisive as the elite media. They put religious, race, ethnic, social, economic, and political groups against each other as a matter of creating division and foisting their agendas.

Government can profile at will but let the people try.

Of all the systems of government, the one hardest to have is the people's democracy.

When you elect politicians, you elect their advisors and financial investors.

What politicians promise and what they deliver are usually very different.

The oligarchs are every bit the dictator, but less visible with their better cover.

When you are told what to say or not to say for political correctness, it is censorship for political control—not correctness—and freedom is insidiously threatened.

Those who specialize in the practice of politically labeling others have a hidden agenda for control.

Too often, the reputations of people are determined by the agenda media.

The branding of groups by political title should not be written in stone as so many depart from their original identity.

Group guilt is more shameful than individual guilt since, too often, it is the result of the work by mimicking cowards.

Government has an insatiable appetite that, with age, requires more and more feeding.

Not often is the enemy all bad nor the fatherland all good.

Systemic arrogance within government is as debilitating as bureaucratic inefficiency.

You can count on the agenda media to use hindsight to critique their selected targets.

The only guarantee of good government is in the ceaseless management by the people. Otherwise, government only serves itself and its select groups.

One size does not fit all shapes. Nor does one form of government serve all pure cultures.

Bad democratic governments exist because the pools of people are leaderless, un-attentive or naive.

When a country prides itself for having democracy, it is best for the people to understand for whom that democracy exists and for whom it does not.

Those impressed with tall buildings should take care not to be too enamored with the people in them.

Organizations that purport to protect citizens' rights too often only aim to advance their own privileges.

Before joining the ranks, know the difference between the real patriot and the pseudo-claimant on the edge of his seat wanting to profess to the high heavens his loyalty.

Patriotism is an action and not an empty slogan used by so many who falsely parade their love of country.

The political rhetoric one hears on the public air ways is too often than not only self-serving propaganda.

One would be prudent to note that, too often, human rights activists are nothing more than selfish-rights promoters.

The rule of law is indispensable to a nation's function, but more importantly, it is the culture that defines how the law is utilized and delivered.

A corrupt culture will guarantee a corrupt legal, political, economic, and social system.

That political centralization invariably means more control for government and less freedom for the governed is a given.

The belief that democracy is the panacea for perpetual good government is an accepted philosophy for which there is no basis in history.

Centralization plays no political favorites and has no bounds. The more of it there is, the less there is of freedom.

When the environmental climate becomes the focus for political agendas then most of what comes out of the government's mouth is unreliable.

The gullible insist on seeing with their ears and believing themselves to be visual witnesses.

Political parties and their loyal supporters are quick to blame each other for their similar actions.

Those who persist to look with their ears are destined to see only what they hear.

One cannot help but notice the similarity between politicians and the clergy. Each derives its living from contributions while both preach hope.

Too many wars are instigated by aggressive cowards and fought by unsuspecting pawns. They are usually ended by events rather than rational minds.

Wherever there is intrusive government, there is unloving and self-serving paternalism.

Democracy's greatest hurdles are the many thoughtless and disinterested who believe their form of government should run on cruise control.

If anything defines the media, it is their intrusiveness especially when grieving or troubled people need to be left alone.

Freedom of the press should include the freedom to monitor, investigate, and report about the press. No institution is inviolate with media included.

There is a logical reason for everything, except when humans are involved.

No one exploits the power of suggestion better with the masses than the mogul media.

Government's promotion to instill fear within the populace works very well when government's agendas are aimed at herding people like sheep.

Why could anyone who holds dearly individual freedom accept then to exist comfortably with more and more centralized government?

A group not in power is vigilant to limit government control. The same one, when in power, will champion government activism.

Numbers are an exact science and do not lie except when in the hands of agenda activists fondly in the habit of quoting statistics.

The naïve and dishonest believe that their country's duty for going to war is always to protect the nation and maintain the peace.

All too often, the dishonest media will make a hero the bum and a bum the hero.

A country cannot convince the world of its greatness simply by advertising it as such.

Those most susceptible to advertising are also easily controlled by propaganda.

Big advertising's mission for success is to substitute itself as the bearer of reality.

Unbridled corruption is the main ingredient for the failure of any political system. It is the enemy of good government and should be swatted down like infected flies.

Although people generally have to pay for their mistakes, governments rarely do. In both cases, the people are obligated to pick up the pieces.

Beware the tricky saboteur who discredits his adversary only to allow himself to create his own havoc.

Political centralization is the insidious stranglehold used by the elite to control government and corral the people.

Creating chaos is the illegitimate maneuver for gaining undeserved power.

Chaos is the enemy of civilized behavior.

Decency cannot exist in the midst of chaos.

Agenda law is the corrupt weapon for the legal lawless elite.

The transference of societal culture from the village to the city is not so much a gain for good human behavior as it is a windfall for the legal and monetary systems.

Centralization is the enemy and end of free and individual choice.

Climate, a most common matter to humanity's business, is the perfect vehicle for effecting centralized world organizational control.

There is no greater long-term threat to a democratic society than a monolithic agenda-driven media with its power to almost forever control the minds of the general population.

When democratic elections are determined by money and media, then what you have is farcical government.

A peaceful world has no place for radical zealots who claim to have a monopoly on everyone else's salvation.

Do not exclusively reject the heretic as, at times, his heresy comes with merit and serves a common good.

After food, clothing, and shelter, the most necessary requirement for humanity's safety and good health is having a world balance of power.

When government, big media, and big business are aligned together, it matters not the form of government as the people will be deemed too impotent to protect their rights.

You will not have an honest government for long without an honest major media.

When the people are gullible, no form of government will protect them.

Governments are impotent without power.

The governed should understand that their government delivers its powers always by using a two-edged sword.

Democratic political systems are the preferred environments for the elitist oligarchs who find the public much easier to sway than strong unopposed leaders.

The banker makes it his business to use your money to finance his pocket book and pay for his wars.

Much of history is the same lie repeated over and over.

If dictators are often brutal leaders, democratically elected leaders are often abusive political prostitutes.

Democracies are usually anything but what they purport to be as elections are won with media, money, and party organization, not usually with grass roots voter preference.

Modern hyper-fast technology is rapidly creating a centralized world whereby the planet's population could more easily be controlled by a very few. Very little could be more devastating to humanity.

War provides an opening for legal killing that also includes a cover for action of cold blooded, cowardly murder.

Modern history is no more reliable than ancient history only because today's historians' skewed reporting supersedes technology's ability to capture the facts.

"1984" has made its way over into the twenty-first century, bedded its-self down and grown.

"Do as I say not as I do" must have been coined by ubiquitous "holy than thou" religious and political leaders.

Any form of highly centralized government, given enough time, will ultimately lead to an oligarchical plutocracy and suffocate the individual's rights.

It is much simpler to feed too many people a gift wrapped lie than to convey to them a bare boned truth.

Governments that rely on guile or force more readily than sincerity are destined to create chaos for their citizens.

A world government will insure world servitude.

Simple folk can be as smart as those who are more sophisticated. The sophisticate, however, is just more adept at being intellectually devious.

The first indication of the loss of freedom is when select subjects cannot be mentioned or debated openly.

Those who cannot discern the hypocrite will not easily protect their own interests.

When not fighting for a cause, the soldier must be given something to hate or fear in order to accomplish his leaders' mission.

The fool outnumbers the sage and the exploiter is ready to exploit.

Know the difference between the soldier who fights for his country and the one who just enjoys the exercise.

Anyone not privy to a politician's inner circle should not take what he says publically as being a sincere reflection of his belief or intention.

While the honorable soldier offers his life and limb in battle, the dishonorable banker and politician welcome the opportunity for wealth and power.

Nothing is more senseless than an unnecessary war and nothing more worthwhile than the insistence upon peace.

There may be no greater coward than the activist warmonger who knows he will never see a battlefield.

Democracy is easy to sell, but difficult to deliver.

Those who want their government to provide for all their needs and solve all their problems are trading paternalism for servitude.

Debates and warnings are but little ammunition when competing against the big guns of well-placed money and organization by those seeking power.

"Too big to fail" means nothing more than too big are held accountable.

We can discern much about our media by the choice of information they decide to pass on to us, and by what they omit or distort.

If we hesitate to send our youth into battle when the cause is just, how do we justify sending them to war when meritless?

Whenever a subject is deemed "politically incorrect," but not constitutionally, it is merely an insidious ploy to impose censorship.

Whoever intends to control the mass media conspires to manipulate the minds of the general population to influence and rule by guile.

The power to monopolize the media delivers enormous power to monopolize the thinking of the public.

If we are to accept a monolithic world government, then we surely will become a centralized world of serfs to those directing this unified government.

The manipulative media are as destructive as dangerous weapons.

A politician's sincerity is as good as his promises during an election campaign.

If the manipulated inhabitants of society could know how their exploiters disrespect their cluelessness, they would revolt.

When a government propagandizes its inhabitants more than citizens in other countries, then its institutions are disloyal to its people.

Propaganda works when the brain doesn't.

The unquestioning believer seeks comfort while the sceptic looks for truth.

A government that deceives its people is a government that will steal from them and not just their money.

The special interest lobbyist is a parasite of no constructive purpose. He fosters corruption at the highest level sadly from those positioned to act for the common good.

Used car salesmen have not the capacity to misrepresent as much as the lobbyists, who are paid much more.

The most constructive or destructive possession in the hands of the enforcer is his humanity or lack thereof.

Freedom, once established, is not a commodity that automatically resets itself in order to stay on course.

Erosion begins unnoticed and continues as such until the foundation falls. So it is with corrupt government.

The people should be the ones to judge what is socially acceptable or "politically correct"—not the government, nor the elite media, nor any political groups, and certainly not some self-appointed band of plutocrats.

The politics of giving has nothing to do with the sincerity of giving. The former rarely goes to the deserving while the latter has a better chance of reaching the needy.

Too much of the mass media's daily "reporting" as fact and accepted by the general public will not stand the test of truth in a courtroom.

One country's sanctions against another's are an act of war and are meant to create suffering on its innocent inhabitants to cause internal strife or revolution.

The trick in life is to look through the obvious to discern one's real enemy masking itself in the open or hiding in the shadows while realizing the warmth of a true friend.

Endowing one group's rights over another's is a formula for social and political upheaval.

The best way for world control is to find something continuously central to the interests of every human being—the climate. It is the new politic posing as science for the purpose of fulfilling an agenda.

The cowardly schemer will invariably choose to buy off his enemies rather than negotiate with or challenge them. So it is with nations.

Two types of people are certain about their conclusions. They are the well informed and the utterly ignorant.

Easy money erodes good character while reinforcing the bad.

The citizenry should make it their business to be aware of pressrooms in order to discern news reporting from disinformation.

When someone is shown to be depressed and alluding to suicide, those near and dear are advised to take it at face value.

There is a need to find another word for budget when used to describe government spending.

The bigger the government, the smaller is the freedom.

Whoever controls what we read and hear will have the upper hand to control much of what we believe.

Reporters who make it their business or cause to expose other's misdeeds will never report on themselves.

Many revolutions are more a reaction for a grievance rather than a conspiracy without merit. The people must make it their business to know the difference.

Freedom of speech is not a privilege to be defined and dispensed by select persons, groups, or institutions. It is that indispensable mandate for all to enjoy. Without this precious right to speak out, all other freedoms will eventually fall.

Popular stories of war are most always shot full of holes.

Whoever writes societies' rules holds the cards to insure control of the game.

Warmonger governments are not interested in outside opinions of their righteousness, but only whether they have the unquestioned and continuing support of their populace.

Big capitalism employs the same vices and commits the same sins as big government.

When big media and its reporters are propaganda outlets and writers for their own ends, then they serve not the public but only themselves.

Freedom of the press is non-existent when a self-serving culture of information manipulators replaces factual reporters.

When the media are generally on the same page as government, then this collusion is suspect at best.

Those unquestioning supporters of well-meaning causes for which they know little or nothing are the dupes of society.

Too many politicians are insincere schemers who have been made to appear as heroes.

Wagering on a long shot horse to win guarantees a more favorable set of odds than betting on the fulfillment of a politician's promises.

I can think of a no more evenly matched contest than one that pits used car salesmen vs politicians.

Entertainment media have a way of making celebrities out of some people who merely smile and move about.

The beggar is more worthy of a free lunch than the hypocritical political or religious leader.

Corrupt governments employ meaningless investigations to show that something is being done to protect the public interest. They go nowhere except to satisfy the naïve inhabitants.

When you meet an honest, humble politician, put a warm blanket around him so as to help protect him from his peers.

Freedom of speech for all is not cheap. Turning one's head rather than defending it costs nothing.

Centralization deals more with control than with efficiency. Governments that promote it mean to increase their rule.

Know the guilty from the scapegoat or forever be at risk.

There is no treachery so grave as a traitor who will scapegoat an innocent to blame for that which he is accountable.

A country's constitution cannot be momentarily set aside in the interest of national security. Without it there is no national security.

When wars are fought by older rather than younger men, then and only then will we have less of these destructive upheavals.

Constitutional rights do not come with exceptions. They are either in process for all or are in jeopardy for all.

In war, the victor in a time not long down the road often fairs no better than the vanquished. This says much for the futility of war.

Know those who espouse peace when they are the underdog, but whom readily make war when they have the upper hand.

The first order of business for a politician is to request money for election and when once elected to just keep asking.

The statesman endows himself with fortitude and courage, while the politician comes with an innate hypocrisy and guile.

Too often, the politician is promoted or mistaken as a statesman.

Democratic elections give the people the solemn right to vote their preference of who will take their money.

It is not enough to discern ones action but equally as important to know the history behind the action.

It seems that too many lawyers are no better for a society than too few.

When government and big media consistently are on the same page, then one should not believe what either disseminates.

Global centralization has all the ear markings for world serfdom.

If the people allow, government will govern the filet for itself and leave the chuck for its citizenry.

Government is a club. Those inside deem the rest as outsiders.

Government's checks and balances on itself are not enough. The people must have their own eyes and hands on government.

The truly valiant are those very few who will stand against an ill-meaning social or political tide when all others will not.

Any political system that relies almost exclusively on lobby money and a propaganda media for electoral success is anything but democratic.

War is the ultimate insult imposed upon those who have to fight it by those who don't.

Not to have suffered is not to have tasted the depth of life.

Nothing puts a nation more at harm than a growing corruption allowed to build up to become a way of life.

Whoever coined the phrase "Do as I say, not as I do" must have had some preachers and politicians in mind.

A lame duck government is not nearly as ineffectual as a lame duck citizenry.

Corruption is the meal that governments like to feed to their people.

While the elected know their constituents opinions of them, those voters have little clue of how they are viewed by those they elected.

To control the media is to control the misinformation given and the information not given to the public.

The promoters of "politically correct" are manipulators who want society to march to their beat.

Power is derived from having superior control of force or money. To possess both is to have true power.

When a people lose the ability to think for themselves, democracy has no influence or relevance.

While the pen is mightier than the sword, the television is mightier than both.

Big media today is most sophisticated propaganda weapon.

Technology has given humanity the power now to easily annihilate itself and by all indications that appears to be the plan.

When big media uses their power of the word and the camera to advance their own social and political agendas, then they abuse their freedom and should be brought to account.

Too many holy leaders forget to follow what they preach to the flock.

No matter how misrepresented or tainted, call it a foundation and the public will buy into it—no questions asked.

Better to have holy men who would practice what they preach rather than have those who would preach that which they practice.

Too often, conscience surfaces in the minds of men soon or long after their misdeeds. And, too often, conscience returns to sleep again in the minds of men while similar misdeeds are repeated.

The reasons for anti-gun laws preferred by citizens and those by government are very much apart.

When the law is corrupted, what follows is the turning of criminal action into legal activity.

The power to control the media message is the power to control the way people think and act. It is a power that can modify cultures. This control is the feeding tube for misinformation, false interpretation, insidious brain washing, and hiding truth.

Shame is a most honest and noble feeling.

When a foreign army comes to a country to be the owner of the land and all life upon it, then how does this intruder really expect to be received as a beloved?

Whenever a government empowers some, it disempowers others.

The less convention is allowed to be the driving factor in the working of society the more the emphasis is placed upon the law to inforce the peace. When the balance is tipped too far in favor of policing by legal enforcement rather than social convention, the more will be the recipe for injustice.

The past is not alive and only functions as a memory. The present is what breathes now and the future can only wait to be born.

Democracy under a self-serving government is a myth. Those that believe in it are the food and fuel by which democracies cannot exist.

When truth is most vital is when truth is unpopular or not in demand.

Accountability is what delivers the attractiveness of democracy to its people. Without accountability, democracy is impotent or a mere wishful thought.

Democracy only guarantees freedom when the people control their elected representatives and not the reverse.

Centralization is the enemy of civilization. It robs culture of its variety, society of its differences, persons of their uniqueness, and insures efficiency of control.

It is vital to a country's health that the people recognize an organized agenda media who will manipulate moles into mountains and mountains into moles.

While technology has done much to heal or cure diseases of the body and brain, it has done nothing to insure a healthier mind.

Political parties will not hesitate to select and support even the devil for office if the devil fits their mold and can advance their interests.

The legal profession's "deep pockets" rationale is not only greed-based, it often transfers culpability from the blameful to the blameless.

Equality is not to be confused for equity nor equity for equality. The naïve and lazy minded allow the exploiters to miss-define their use to achieve their own purposes.

Pure democracy is unbridled permissiveness and becomes anarchy. It can only flourish if humanity is errorless.

To understand humanity is to realize that one man's devil is another's angel.

The banker enjoys a different set of rules for protecting his money than does the man on the street.

To believe one's political party preference is always cleaner than the other's is to believe one's child is always more angelic than rest.

The politician's duty to be beholden to his monetary sponsors and satisfy the media while deceiving the voter insults democracy.

To believe simply that the law simply equates with justice is simply quite simple minded.

Political globalism is the excuse for world domination.

Societies have an obligation to protect the positive aspects of their culture such as truth, honesty, respect, and integrity. Whenever outside influence immigrates into such societies, the people must stop any foul, foreign habits in their tracks. To allow otherwise is to allow constructive society to be corrupted and only when they wake will the people realize that they have become base.

Until every human is born, an angel with all that is desired guaranteed to each, then no political or economic system will satisfy for long.

There exists no system of government that can protect its people from unscrupulous or compromised leadership.

Intellect is no guarantee of good judgement.

Today's hero can be tomorrow's outcast and vice-versa.

The record of psychiatry's success in treating the mentally ill is dismal and borders on false advertisement for claiming to be an equal arm of medicine.

The trick in life is to discern opinion from fact.

When democracy elects the best chatterer, with the best banker, and with the most media, then what you have is anything but a government of the people.

In politics, there comes a time when even the feeblest of people have had enough of bad government.

Perverted government can flourish within any political system. Democracy is not an exception.

The naïve and gullible are the grist for any politician's mill.

Nothing ensures peace more than a balance of power. Nothing ensures war more than a monopolistic media.

To believe that elections are rigged under dictatorships and not under democracies is to believe in fairy tales.

Movies are the corrupters of history.

Until there comes a better way to elect officials other than with money and media, the guarantee of political corruption will characterize most leaders.

There can be no good government without an honest and independent legal system.

The principle failing of democracy is its reliance on the public's acumen to elect the right person.

The promotion of democracy as a foreign policy has become nothing more than a ploy to replace foreign governments we do not like with the ones we do.

Successful bureaucrats make good bureaucratic decisions, but too often miss the mark in finding simple, sense driven solutions.

Bureaucracy is the bane of efficiency.

When in a democracy, the irresponsible come to outnumber the responsible, then one should rue the outcome of one man, one vote.

A successful country must allow water to seek its own level or it will not remain successful for long.

The success of any political system is not within its makeup but in its leadership and the people's reaction to it.

A one-party only corrupt political system is better than a two-party as political corruption needs no competition.

Money and fire are very much akin. Both are constructive servants but destructive masters.

Centralize the world and you centralize power. Centralize power and you centralize serfdom.

Humans being what they are mean wars exist and will continue to do so.

A society that thinks one way privately and speaks another publically can only become a hypocrite unto itself.

Politics, too often, befits more the outhouse than the office.

The more centralized a government, the less free its people.

It is best to avoid dealing with the arrogant when possible as arrogance is the enemy of good conscience and even good sense.

How is it that some of our most religious citizenry are too often some of the most itching to go to war?

One cannot reason with those who possess blind faith stupidity.

Little exists that is viler than institutional injustice.

A marriage without love continues to be viable as long as husband and wife stay accustomed to each other.

To age in life is to move from chair to chair. With it, our perspective seems to alter as we change positions.

Good judgement dictates not parading ones bank account, religion, or politics.

With the ignorant and gullible, any conceivable injustice is possible.

The ignorant and gullible are the perfect prey for the manipulator's agenda.

Ignorance is the main obstacle in the quest for reason and progress.

The authors of "politically correct' are those who blamelessly wish to control freedom of thought and speech.

War can turn the most civil human into the basest animal.

It matters not to the politician his intent or belief, but only what the voter will buy.

Nothing speaks more to the salesmanship of a select few and the gullibility of the many than the success of the diamond industry.

Those that are arrogant and ignorant are incapable of just decisions.

The agenda centralist wants it all in one pot so he can better control what's in it.

Humanity's biggest problem is that not enough are capable of thinking for themselves.

Dictators rule by strength and wits. The elected do so by pleasing their benefactors.

Nothing fills an equine outhouse more than a politician's promises.

It is the court's duty to get at the truth no matter where it leads. Its duty is to do it by not turning its head from facts, nor avoiding controversy, or giving special treatment of anyone.

The successful prevaricator knows that if he lies vehemently and often enough that it will become so.

Technology is both the reliever and the enslaver.

Politicians are the last people to invite in if veracity is what you seek.

No man is a god so we should treat none as such.

Do not look to politicians for the truth.

Right or wrong, the world belongs to the persistent activist.

Politically correct has no place where free speech exists.

Religion is politics. Not to understand it makes one vulnerable to believe in religion without discerning its political agenda.

The politician will promise you whatever you wish for a vote. Once elected, he will do whatever he wants.

Commercial advertising is the enemy of reality.

A vilest injustice is a government that shelters its employees from punishment no matter the crime.

Centralization is the most efficient means for putting the populace under one's thumb.

What makes war so popular is that God is on everyone's side.

If the people have neither the time nor inclination to study, what are the government and self-interest organizations agendas then? They should not expect to be represented.

Human frailty makes it impossible for democracy to last.

War is organized and wholesale murder supported by good citizens.

Until the majority of electorate can think for themselves, democracy is no more possible than someone hugging their shadow.

To control the media is to monopolize the way people think and the way matters seem.

On media reporting, ask the question, "Why is it happening this way and does it make sense?"

Democracy is also an undesirable form of government for an ill-informed and inept populous.

Outside negative interventions by force or guile imposed upon other societies are the cancers by which cultures are forever eroded.

The agenda media specialize in erecting false houses and razing solid foundations.

Democracies can become as controlled and corrupt as dictatorships.

It is the people and only they who can protect themselves against their government.

If some do not know how to prevaricate, then they must learn in order to be a reporter, lawyer or politician.

The spoils of war will come at a price; if not upon victory, then at a time beyond the peace.

Lasting democracy exists in the minds of dreamers and in the story books.

Technology's rewards are many, but exact a price on culture.

Preachers are to their congregations what politicians are to their constituents. Each is adept at fleecing their flock.

Our law makers are too often our law breakers.

Democracy is neither for the naïve, the gullible, nor a society at odds with itself. It requires political intellect and consensus.

The obvious needs no clarification. Any of it only invites confusion.

Faith is personal while religion is communal. Why then would one want to believe in what someone else preaches for which no proof exists?

There are two principal types of revolution. One is revolution by revolution—the other revolution by evolution. Each comes with its own fingerprint—one by the use of battle the other by guile. Make no mistake. Both are revolutions in their own right.

Money makes one comfortable, it does not make one rich.

War is organized and wholesale murder supported by good citizens.

While blaming politicians for their actions, remember to include their masters who fund and lobby them.

History will attest that humans being what they are mean wars and that is inevitable.

It is preferable for the voter to expose oligarch government. Let the true rulers of "democratic government" be held responsible for their ruses so even the naïve and disinterested will better know who is really to blame for selecting "democracy's "leadership.

Beware those who profess verbally or feign their patriotism to one government, but dedicate their support to another.

What matters more than a nation's form of political system is the fabric of its people. For here is the true opportunity for a country's success.

A democracy will not survive the demands of a self-interested public who only have an understanding or inclination for a culture of consensus in matters of war.

An undefined press brings into question the qualification for the press' sweeping self-appointed rights under the rights of the common good.

There exists no freedom of speech in a society where political correctness is used as a weapon by government and media to embarrass and punish those who speak their conscience.

Too often, there appears to be little room at the top for people of conscience.

The pendulum is always at work. Not to understand this is not to understand life.

Politics is the art of exposing and blaming others for sins, but hiding and ignoring one's own.

War brings out the worst in us and peace the best. Yet, we insist on each.

Too many will believe anything they are told if it is preached hard enough, spoken loud enough, repeated long enough, and insisted vehemently enough.

—MICHAEL G. MERHIGE

CPSIA information can be obtained
at www.ICGtesting.com
Printed in the USA
FSHW04n1354170318
45798FS

9 781633 385825